AF413634

How to Become a US Citizen

US Government Textbook

Children's Government Books

Throughout history lots of people have immigrated from other countries to the United States. They can become United States citizens by going through the legal process below. Many people want to become United Citizens because of the rights and possibilities that are available in this great country.

What is a citizen?

It identifies your national origin. It defines your rights and responsibilities to the country in which you were born. Most people are only a citizen of one country, but it is possible to have dual nationality. Citizens of the United States are either native-born, foreign-born, or naturalized. All of these U.S. citizens owe their loyalty to the United States and are allowed its protection.

US street view

Why become a U.S. citizen?

There are many reasons that people want to become citizens of the United States. Citizens have the right to vote in all federal elections. Some states may deny this right to people that are convicted felons. They have a right to a U.S. passport. This will allow them to not only travel internationally, in several cases without the need of a visa, and also grants the freedom to reenter the United States.

They may be able to petition to bring their family members to the U.S. They can file for a green card, for their spouse, siblings, parents, and children. These are known as the Immediate Relative Immigrant Visas and Family Preference Immigrant Visas. The Immediate Relative visas are unlimited, which means that the relative will only experience a short wait time to obtain their green card and not have to wait for availability of a visa. Permanent residents can petition only for their children and spouses, not their siblings or parents, and these visas are limited.

PROVED
sa
Approved
Denied

Even though holding a green card provides the holder with permanent immigrant status, the possibility exists that they could be deported for committing a major crime or other similar reasons. A citizen holds a stronger place in our society and cannot be deported.

to the
United States
New

Department of Homeland Security
DENT CARD

Department of Homeland Security
SIDENT CARD

Children of citizens have right to citizenship. Any person born here automatically becomes a citizen. Even when born abroad, a child can still claim U.S. citizenship by a process of registering his birth before turning 18. Even if a child does not claim their citizenship prior to his 18th birthday, he can become a citizen through the naturalization process.

Citizenship in the United States affords a person the opportunity to obtain funds for education. We have one of the most renowned education systems, particularly when it comes to university and colleges. As a citizen, you have the right to grants issued by the government for education, a right that you would not have as a permanent resident. Most of the scholarships issued by schools and private institutions require that the student by a citizen.

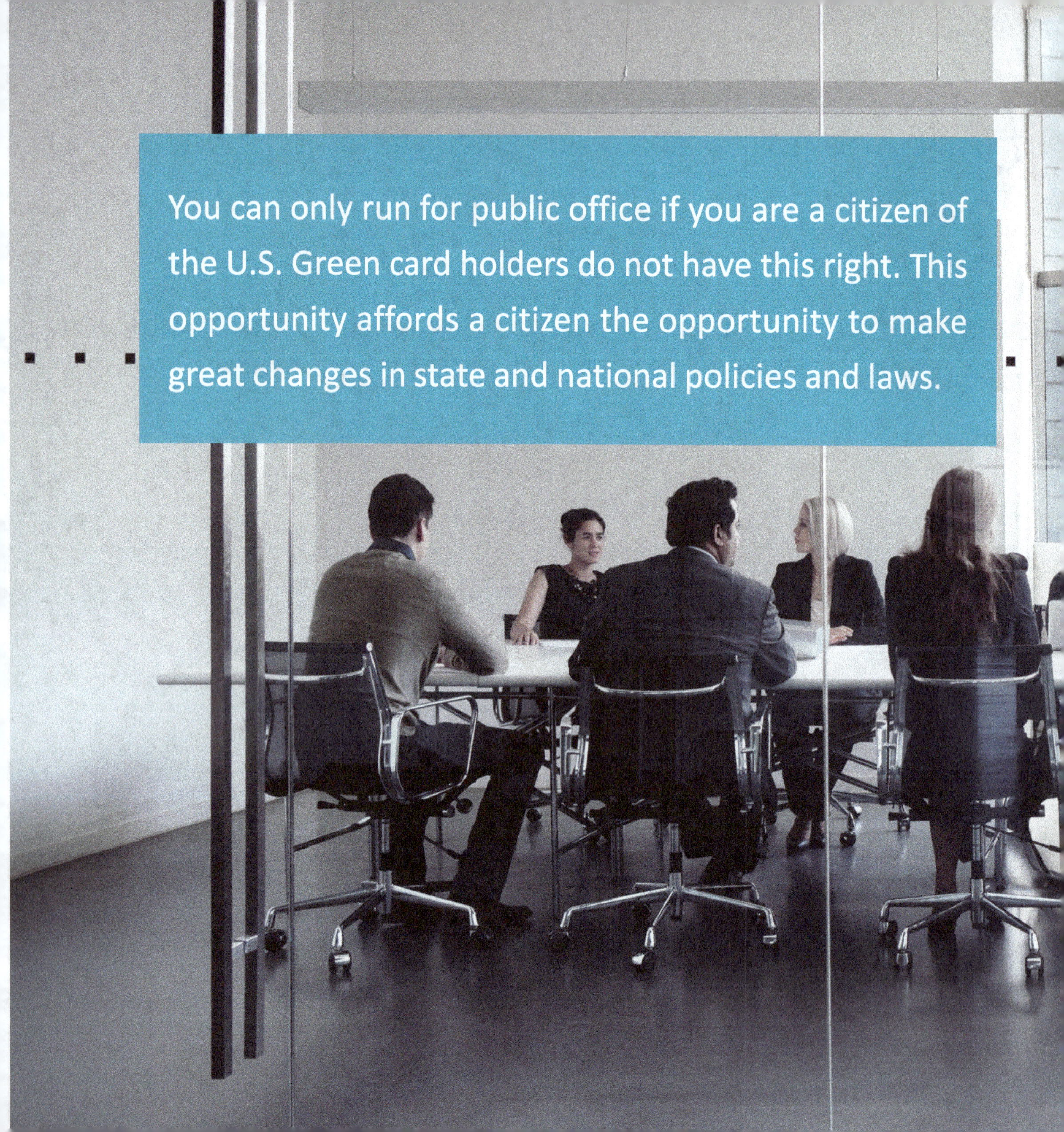

You can only run for public office if you are a citizen of the U.S. Green card holders do not have this right. This opportunity affords a citizen the opportunity to make great changes in state and national policies and laws.

We never forget
that half of a
↑ Customer Service Center
⌡ Telephones
↑ ✈ Terminals 2 3 5
Concourses B E F
Gates C1–C19 C
🧳 Baggage Claim
Ground Transport
Gate C20
10:59
It's time to fly.
It's time to fly.
↙ ✈ Terminals
Concourses B E
Baggage Claim
Ground Transport
Hilton
Gates C18,C18a
Customer Service
Center
→
It's time to fly.
Telephones
10:59
10:59
C17
C2
Terminal 2
Concourse
Down Escalator
Baggage
Side
CAUTION
at the Airport

As a citizen, you will not lose your citizenship status, no matter how long you travel abroad. This is quite different for permanent residents as their status would be considered as abandoned and they would lose their green card if they travel abroad for any great length of time. They would not able to come back to the United States.

The Best
Benefits
Plus
3512 7713 8744 0000
5422
VALID THROUGH 09/20

The U.S. government provides many benefits that are available only to citizens. An example would be that a citizen would have the right to full Social Security benefits and a permanent resident would only have right to half. Citizens also are eligible to file for welfare and food stamp benefits.

There are some great jobs working for the federal government in the United States and these are available only to its citizens. FBI agents, postal workers, and court clerks are a few examples of federal jobs. They offer great benefits, great salaries, and often include incredible pensions.

VOTE
HERE
POLLING PLACE

As a citizen of the United States you have undeniable rights. You can vote in an election, work for the government, run for public office, and are safeguarded by the U.S. laws.

Who can become a citizen?

A person must first immigrate legally to the United States and live here five years at least. A Green Card is what an immigrant applies for to become a permanent resident. They must be 18 years old at least, be able to understand and speak English, have a good moral character, and be willing to take the oath of loyalty the United States.

Parents of children under 18 can file an application on behalf of their child to become a naturalized citizen.

Approximately 680,000 people become legal U.S. citizens each year.

Munich
23:35
23:40
Adelaide
23:40
23:45   Los Angeles
23:45   London LHR
23:45   Paris
23:50
23:55
23:55   Sydney
23:55   London LHR
23:55   Frankfurt
20:15
20:25
20:30
20:30
20:35
20:40
20:40
20:40
20:45
20:45
20:45
20:50
20:55
20:55
21:00
21:00
21:05
21:05

The Application Process

Once they are eligible for citizenship, they complete the application N-400. This is sent to the United States Citizenship and Immigration Services (USCIS) to be processed. This can take a long time, sometimes it might take longer than a year, for the processing of the application.

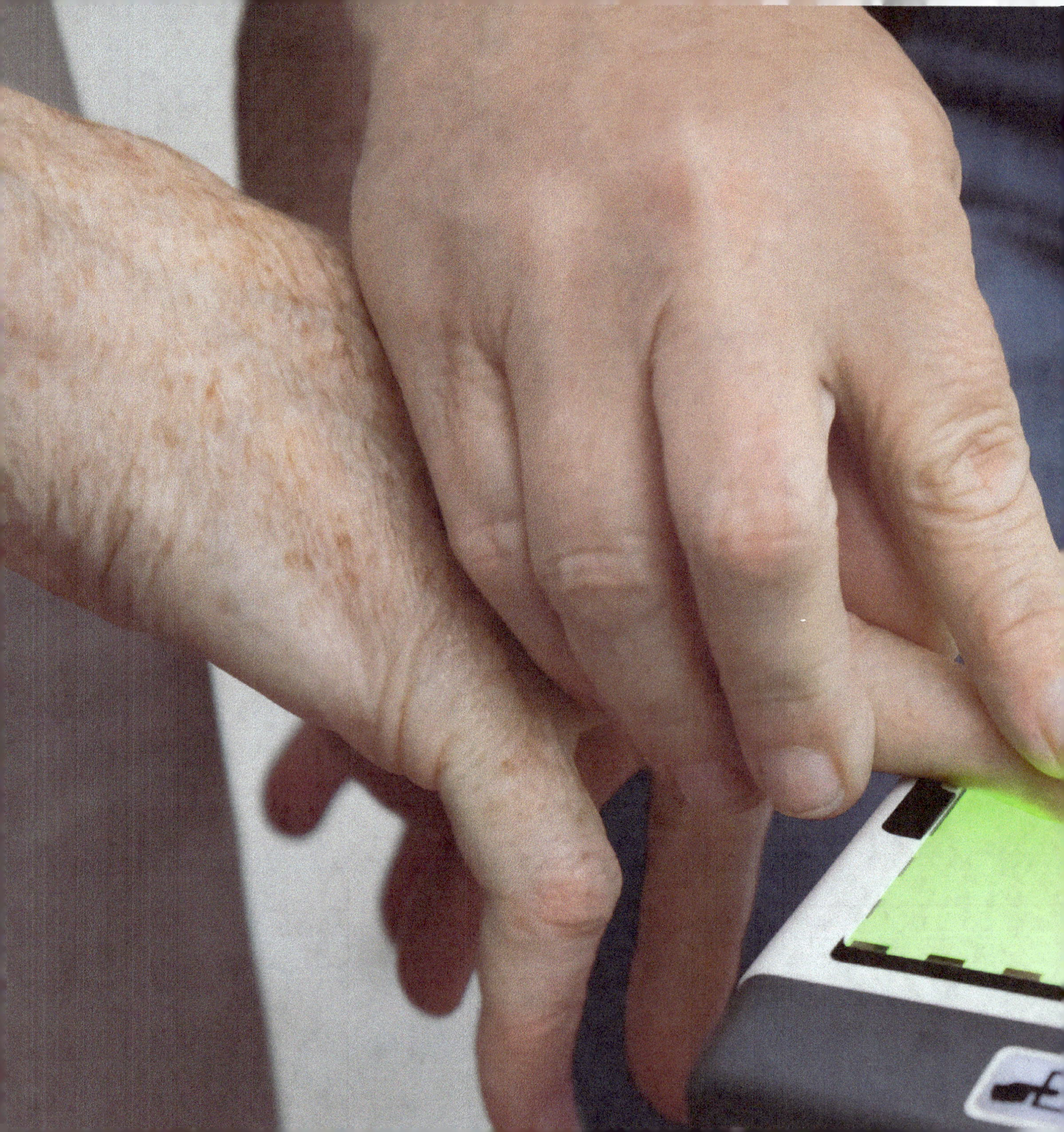

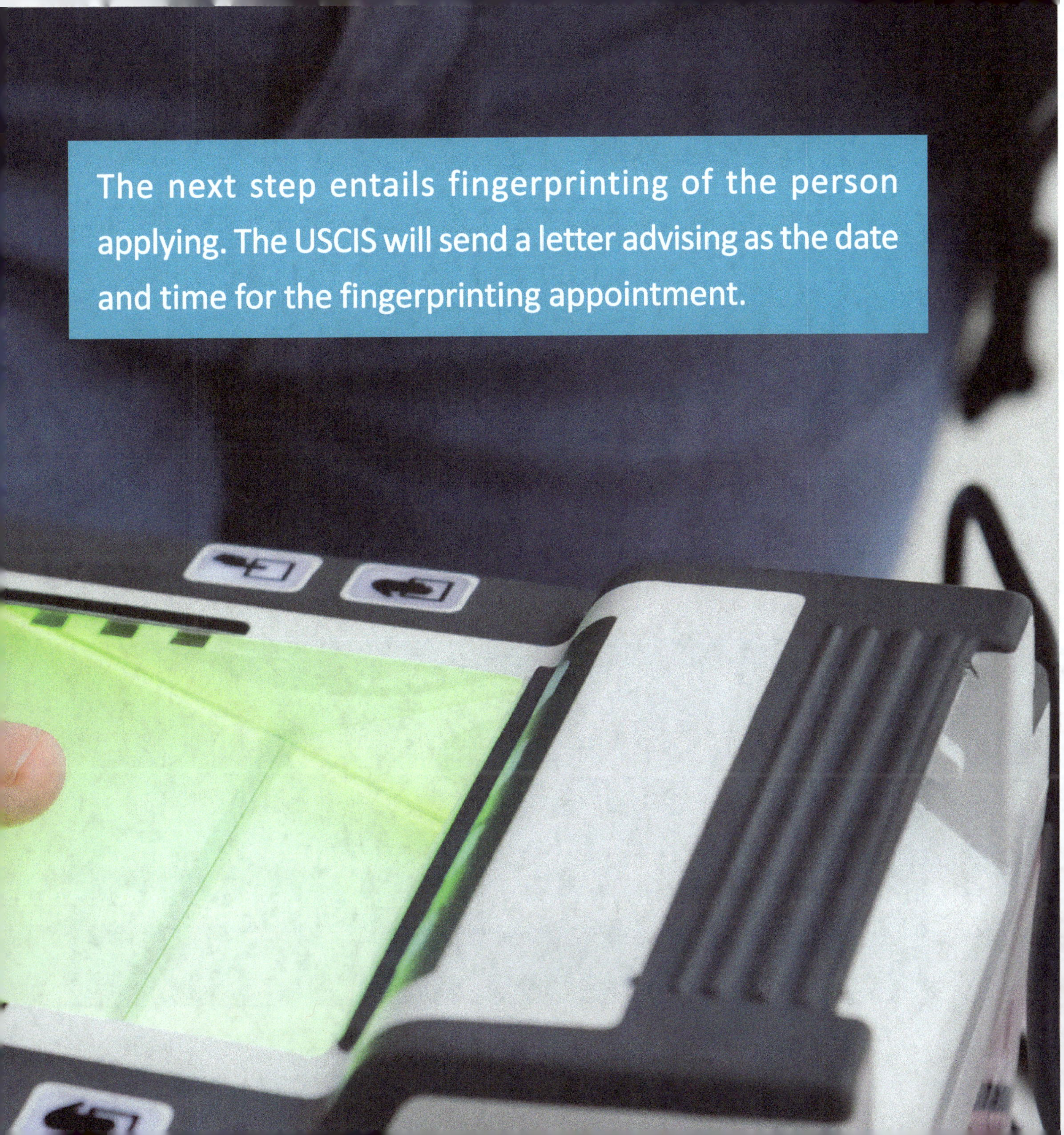
The next step entails fingerprinting of the person applying. The USCIS will send a letter advising as the date and time for the fingerprinting appointment.

At that appointment, they will have to complete a form indicating why the fingerprinting is being done, such as whether it is for citizenship, green card, permanent resident, etc. While most sites still use ink for fingerprinting, eventually it will be done by electronic means.

NTION
Court
SO AMERICA
CITIZENSHIP
inches:
of me.
S. R. LITTLE
RING

The USCIS will then send the fingerprints to the FBI for processing. The FBI will process these fingerprints to check out their background and confirm that they have not committed any major crime.

Occasionally they will be rejected because the quality of the prints was not good. They will then reschedule the appointment and take the fingerprints again.

Police Officer

If for some reason the prints are rejected more than once, you will be asked to provide clearances by police for any places you may have lived.

They will then be interviewed by an officer from the immigration department. They will ask personal questions regarding their background, job, family, and home. Then they will test them to check their ability to understand English. They are also tested on their knowledge of United States history. There is a group of about 100 questions that may be asked.

The applicant is provided with the questions and is given time to study ahead of time.

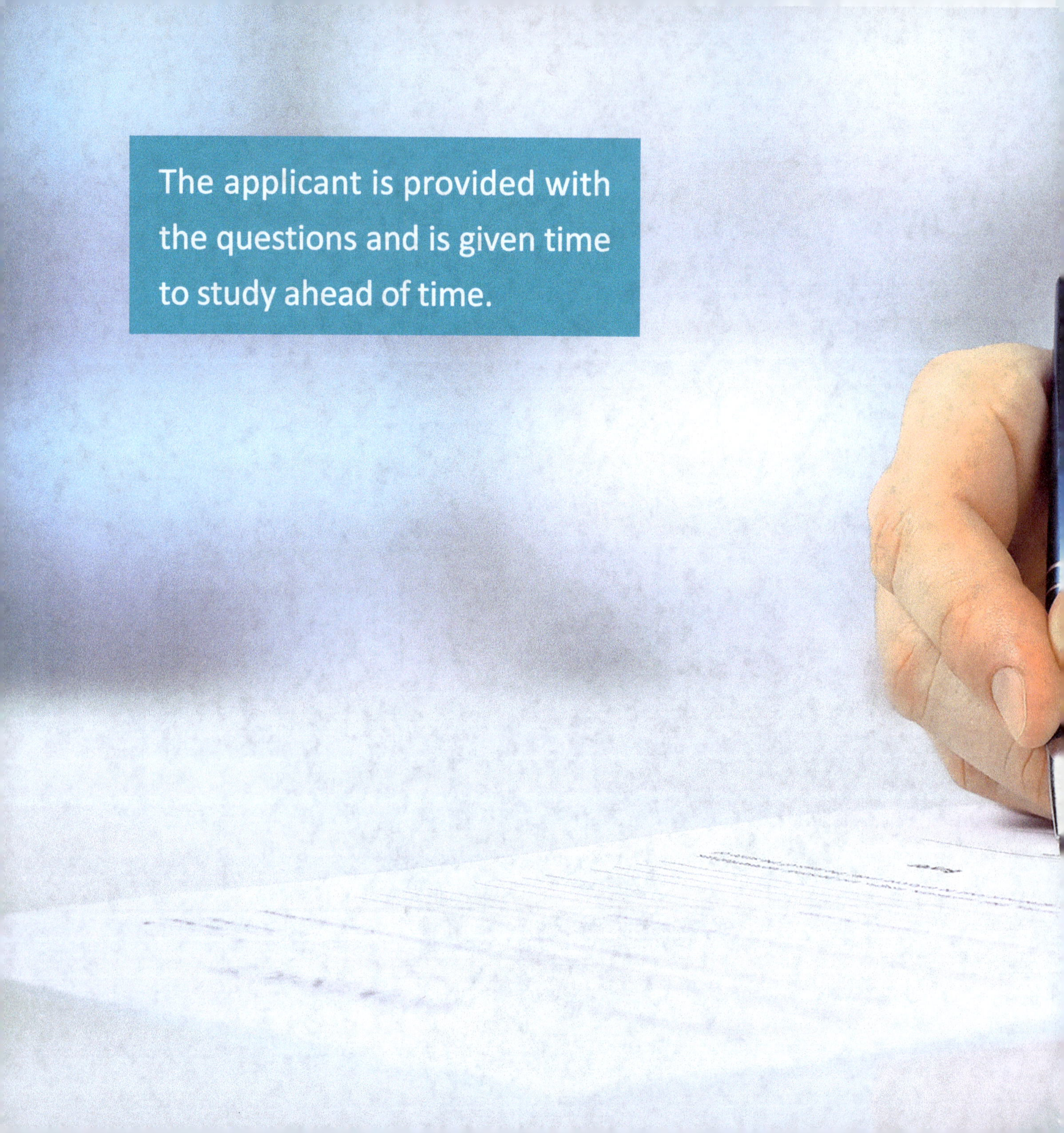

Here are a few questions that someone being interviewed may be asked:

What is known as the supreme law of the land?

What is an amendment?

Who takes charge of our executive branch?

What two parts does the U.S. Congress consist of?

How many Senators are there in the U.S.?

Do you know the answers to these questions? If you don't, you might want to do some research to find out the answers.

Taking the Oath

Once they have passed these requirements, they will then take the Oath of Allegiance, as the last step in becoming a citizen. This is typically done is a courtroom with several other people taking the oath. Once this is done they officially become a U.S. Citizen and receive their Certificate of Naturalization.

Dual Citizenship or Nationality

A person has dual citizenship or nationality when they are a citizen of the United States as well as being a citizen of another country. The United States does not require a person to choose one over another.

PASSPORT
United States
of America

日本
国旅

The United States had banned dual citizenship previously. However, the U.S. Supreme Court, in 1967, repealed most of the law that forbid dual citizenship. The government of the U.S., however, remained scornful of dual citizenship for a long time. Even now, applicants for citizenship of the United States through naturalization are required to relinquish their prior citizenship during the naturalization ceremony.

SPORT
ublic of
United States
of America

The relinquishing of a person's prior citizenship is a part of the oath that new citizens have to take, and if they fail to respect that oath, it may result in the loss of their U.S. citizenship.

As most countries do acknowledge the United States' Oath of Allegiance as being a mandatory contract concerning one's citizenship status, some countries have indicated that this oath does not affect their laws. The government of the U.S. previously would aggressively track these types of cases to get the citizens that were considered as dual citizens to relinquish their citizenship, but they no longer do this.

We The People

The government of the United States does recognize that dual nationality exists, but it does not encourage it because of problems that it might cause. Other countries' claims on the U.S. dual nationals may be in conflict with laws of the United States, and it might limit the U.S. Government's effort to assist nationals that may be abroad. The country where the national is located would typically have a greater claim to that person's allegiance.

For additional information on becoming a United States Citizen be sure to research the internet, go to your local library, and ask questions of your teachers, family, and friends.

Visit
BABY PROFESSOR
EDUCATION KIDS
www.BabyProfessorBooks.com
to download Free Baby Professor eBooks
and view our catalog of new and exciting
Children's Books